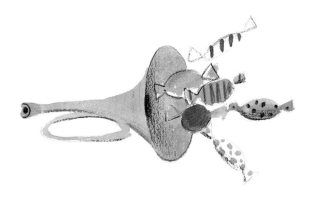

by CARON LEE COHEN

HAPPY to YOU!

illustrated by
ROSANNE LITZINGER

Clarion Books • New York

Clarion Books
a Houghton Mifflin Company imprint
215 Park Avenue South, New York, NY 10003

www.houghtonmifflinbooks.com

Printed in Singapore

Library of Congress Cataloging-in-Publication Data
Cohen, Caron Lee.
Happy to you! / by Caron Lee Cohen ; illustrated by Rosanne Litzinger.
p. cm.
Summary: A baby takes the happiness that he experiences at a
birthday party home with him.
ISBN 0-618-04229-6
[1. Babies—Fiction. 2. Mother and child—Fiction.
3. Happiness—Fiction.] I. Litzinger, Rosanne, ill. II. Title.
PZ7.C65974 Hap 2001
[E]—dc21   99-039433

TWP 10 9 8 7 6 5 4 3 2 1

For Daniel and his mommy—C.L.C.

To Mickey—R.L.

The day Daniel went to Sue's house,
he saw yellow balloons floating on spoons
and a happy cat napping in a happy-face hat
and whistles whistling,

6

7

8

and wrappings ripping
and blocks thump-bumping
and the happy cat jumping
and a black truck *brmmmmming,*

and a pink cake twinkle-twinkling
and boys and girls saying, "*Oooooooo!*"
and singing, "Happy Birthday to you ..."

Daniel sang, too, "Happy to you!"

On his way home, Daniel saw mommies
and daddies and babies and dogs
and said, "Happy to you! Happy to you!"

At home Daniel hugged his brown cow named Moo
and said, "Happy to you!"
To the white bunny on his blue book, he said,
"Happy to you!"
To Daniel in the mirror, he said, "Happy to you!"

Daniel ran out the back door.
"Happy to you!" he said to his big green yard.
And Mommy said, "Happy to you, big blue sky."
"Happy to you, slidey slide," Daniel said.
"Happy to you, bally ball."

Wssssshhhhh went the wind.
And Mommy said, *"Wssssshhhhh."*
"Happy to you, wishedy wind," Daniel said.

Wind wiggled the trees, wiggledy, wiggledy, flippity leaves.
And Mommy said, "Happy to you, flippity leaves."
"Happy to you, lippity leaves," Daniel said.

Chirp, chirp, chirp in the wiggledy trees.
"Happy to you, chirp, chirp, chirp.
Happy to you, wiggledy trees," said Daniel.

22

Wrrrrrrrrrrr in the air.
And Mommy said, "Airplane up there."
"Happy to you, *Wrrrrrrrrrrr*. Happy to you, air,"
Daniel said.

"Happy to you, blue," he told the sky.
"Happy to you, day," he told the world
and waved good-bye.

26

In his room, Daniel's shoes came off.
"Happy to you, offity shoes," he said.
"Happy to you, fresh diaper on," Mommy said.
"Happy to you, freshety shirt," he said.

Mommy put Daniel in his bed. "Naptime," she said.
There was a little word, *no*, in his head.
But instead he said, "Happy to you, naptime.
Happy to you, Mommy."
"Happy to you, Daniel!" she said,
and she kissed his nose and fingers and toes.
"Happy to you, nose and toes," Daniel said.
"Happy to you, sleepy Moo."

And Daniel put his sleepy head
on his soft,
cozy,
comfy pillow,
and closed his eyes, "Happy to ..."

"Sleep," Mommy said.

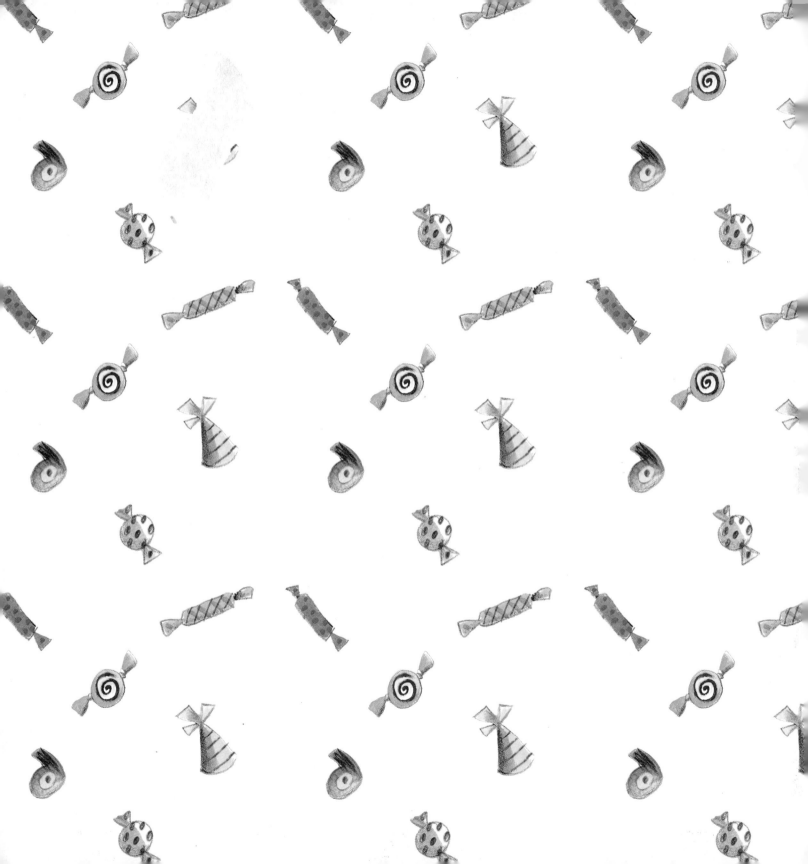